Hello, Family Members,

Learning to read is one of the most important accomplishments of early childhood. **Hello Reader!** books are designed to help children become skilled readers who like to read. Beginning readers learn to read by remembering frequently used words like "the," "is," and "and"; by using phonics skills to decode new words; and by interpreting picture and text clues. These books provide both the stories children enjoy and the structure they need to read fluently and independently. Here are suggestions for helping your child *before, during,* and *after* reading:

Before

- Look at the cover and pictures and have your child predict what the story is about.
- Read the story to your child.
- Encourage your child to chime in with familiar words and phrases.
- Echo read with your child by reading a line first and having your child read it after you do.

During

- Have your child think about a word he or she does not recognize right away. Provide hints such as "Let's see if we know the sounds" and "Have we read other words like this one?"
- Encourage your child to use phonics skills to sound out new words.
- Provide the word for your child when more assistance is needed so that he or she does not struggle and the experience of reading with you is a positive one.
- Encourage your child to have fun by reading with a lot of expression . . . like an actor!

- Have your child keep lists of interesting and favorite words.
- Encourage your child to read the books over and over again. Have him or her read to brothers, sisters, grandparents, and even teddy bears. Repeated readings develop confidence in young readers.
- Talk about the stories. Ask and answer questions. Share ideas about the funniest and most interesting characters and events in the stories.

I do hope that you and your child enjoy this book.

—Francie Alexander
Chief Education Officer,
Scholastic's Learning Ventures

To Sy and Charlie

— L.B.

Go to scholastic.com for web site information on
Scholastic authors and illustrators.

ISBN 0-439-32104-2

Copyright © 2002 by Nancy Hall, Inc.
All rights reserved. Published by Scholastic Inc.
SCHOLASTIC, HELLO READER, CARTWHEEL BOOKS, and associated logos
are trademarks and/or registered trademarks of Scholastic Inc.

Library of Congress Cataloging-in-Publication Data

Hall, Kirsten
        The big sled race / by Kirsten Hall; illustrated by Lindy Burnett.
        p. cm. – (Hello reader! Level 3)
        "Cartwheel books."
        Summary: Two pairs of friends prepare to race each other at the school
sledding contest.
        ISBN 0-439-32104-2 (pbk.)
        [1. Sledding—Fiction. 2. Racing—Fiction.]
        I. Burnett, Lindy, ill. II. Title. III. Series.
        PZ7.H1457 Bi 2002
[E] — dc21   2001032086

10 9 8 7 6 5 4 3   03 04 05 06
                        Printed in the U.S.A.   23
                        First printing, January 2002

The Big Sled Race

by Kirsten Hall
Illustrated by Lindy Burnett

Hello Reader! — Level 3

SCHOLASTIC INC.

New York   Toronto   London   Auckland   Sydney
Mexico City   New Delhi   Hong Kong   Buenos Aires

Mrs. Wong's class was excited.
The big sled race was only one week away!
"I want everyone to find a partner for the race,"
Mrs. Wong said.
Amy looked at Rika, and Rika looked at Amy.
The two friends knew they would be partners.

"And if you like," Mrs. Wong added, "you may decorate your sleds."

"That sounds like fun," Amy said to Rika.

Rika nodded. "I can't wait to decorate ours."

After school Rika and Amy met up with Daniel and Pedro.

Daniel and Pedro were also partners.

"How are you going to decorate your sled?" Rika asked them. "Amy and I are going to add some streamers."

"Decorate our sled?" Pedro said.

"Why would we do a silly thing like that?"

The two boys laughed.

"Oh, never mind them," Amy told Rika.
She put her arm around her best friend.
"You know what, Pedro?" Rika asked.
"We're going to beat you in the race."
Amy nodded. "That's right."

"You are going to beat us?" Pedro laughed.
"That's the funniest thing I've ever heard!"
Rika looked at Pedro. "Amy and I won first place
in the math contest last month," she said.
"But Daniel and I won last week's spelling bee!"
Pedro said.

"Maybe the sledding contest can be our tiebreaker," Daniel said. "Whichever team wins is the all-time champ."

"It's a deal!" Amy said.

The four friends shook hands.

Amy and Rika spent the next week
decorating their sled in Amy's garage.
Rika tied colorful streamers to
the back of their sled.
"Think how pretty this will look as
we zoom down the hill," she said.

Then Amy decided that she wanted to
bring along her doll Belinda.
"Belinda always brings me good luck," she said.
"Well, if you're bringing Belinda, then
I'm bringing my doll Samantha," Rika said.
"And Leo Lion," said Amy. "I must bring Leo."

Soon, the sled was filled with . . .

toys . . .

dolls . . .

stuffed animals . . .

and, of course, extra clothes
in case they got chilly.

The day before the big race,
their sled was finally finished.
"Isn't it great?" Rika asked.
"It's the most wonderful sled I've ever seen!"
Amy agreed. "We're sure to beat Daniel
and Pedro."

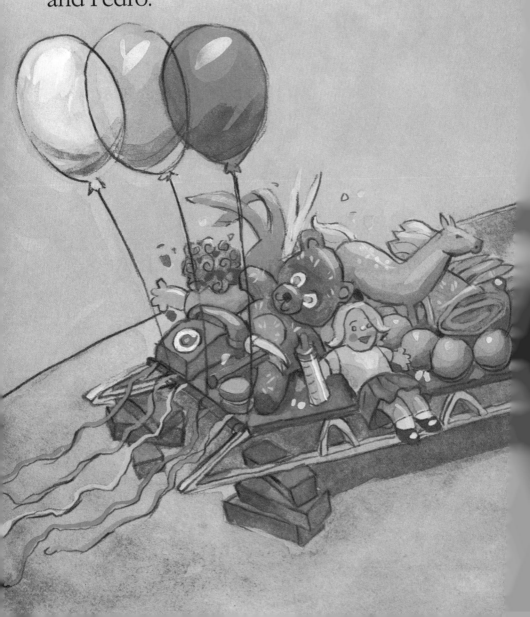

On the day of the race, the girls
pulled the sled to the top of the hill.
They knew that everyone would be
impressed with their hard work.

And everyone was.

Everyone, that is, except for Pedro and Daniel.

"What is that thing?" Pedro said.
"It looks like one of those parade floats."

"Stop it, Pedro," Rika said. "You know very
well that it's our sled."
"You're just jealous," Amy said.
"Jealous?" Pedro said. "Ha!"
"Well, let's see your sled, then!" Amy said.

Daniel and Pedro pointed to their sled.
It was nothing more than a plain plastic saucer.
The only decorations were a few
superhero stickers that Pedro had stuck on.

Amy and Rika smiled at each other.
They knew that their sled looked much better
than Pedro and Daniel's.

Daniel and Pedro smiled at each other, too.
But they were smiling for a different reason.
They knew that the girls had added too much
weight to their sled.
It would never move as quickly as theirs would.

"Those girls are never going to win,"
Daniel told Pedro. "Their sled is too heavy."
"I know," said Pedro. "Then, when they lose,
they'll say it wasn't a fair race."
"Let's give them a head start," Daniel said.
"Good idea," Pedro said.

"Everyone to the starting line,"
Mrs. Wong called out.

"Amy! Rika!" Pedro shouted. "We've decided
to give you a head start. We'll count to ten after
you begin, then we'll take off. And we're still
going to win!"

Mrs. Wong blew the whistle. *TWEEET!*

All the sleds took off down the hill.
All the sleds, that is, except for one.

Pedro began to count. "One. Two. Three. See, Daniel? They're hardly even moving!" Pedro pointed at Amy and Rika who were inching their way down the hill.

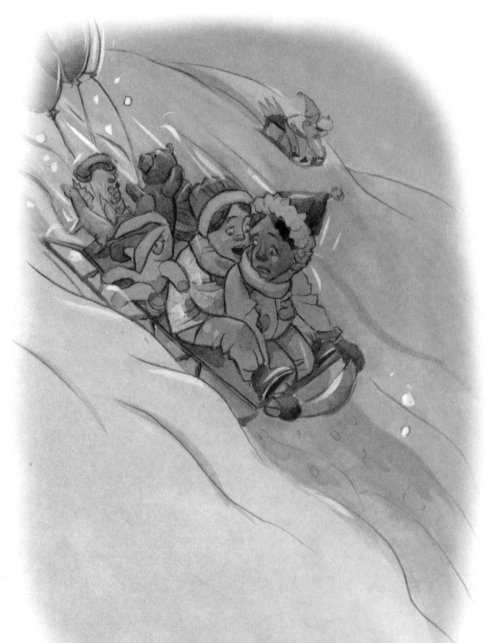

"Why are we moving so slowly?" Amy asked.

"I'm not sure," Rika said, "but I think
we have too much stuff on our sled."

"There's only one way to find out!" Amy said.

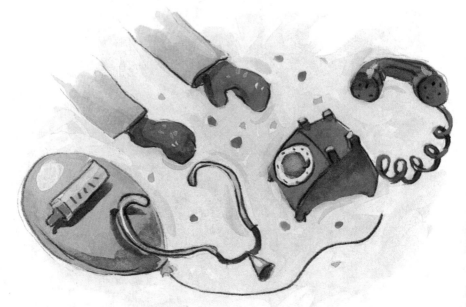

Off flew the toys.

Off flew the dolls and stuffed animals

Off flew the extra clothes.

With each thing they tossed from the sled,
the girls began to pick up speed.

"Uh-oh!" Daniel said to Pedro. "They're getting rid of their things! We'd better move it!" Daniel and Pedro hopped onto their saucer and raced down the hill.

Amy looked back. "The boys are right behind us," she said.

"We've got nothing left to throw off!" Rika said

"We waited too long," Daniel said. "The girls
are going to beat us. They're almost at the
finish line!"

"So are we!" Pedro shouted.

Whoosh! The two sleds crossed the finish line.
"Who won?" Amy asked.

Mrs. Wong stepped up to the finish line. "Congratulations!" she said. "We have a tie for third place."
She handed each team member a ribbon.

After the race, Pedro and Daniel helped Amy
and Rika pick up their toys.
"Now what will we do for the tiebreaker?"
Pedro asked.

"I have an idea . . . " Daniel said.

"One point for us!" Amy called out.
Her snowball sailed right into Pedro.
Pedro threw a snowball at Rika. "Another
point for us!" he said.
"Who's winning?" Daniel asked.
"Who cares?" said Rika. "We're having fun!"